CLARA

the Fortune-Telling Chicken

story and pictures by Ellen Weiss

Windmill Books and E. P. Dutton · New York

for Leatie and Jackie,
best parents in the land

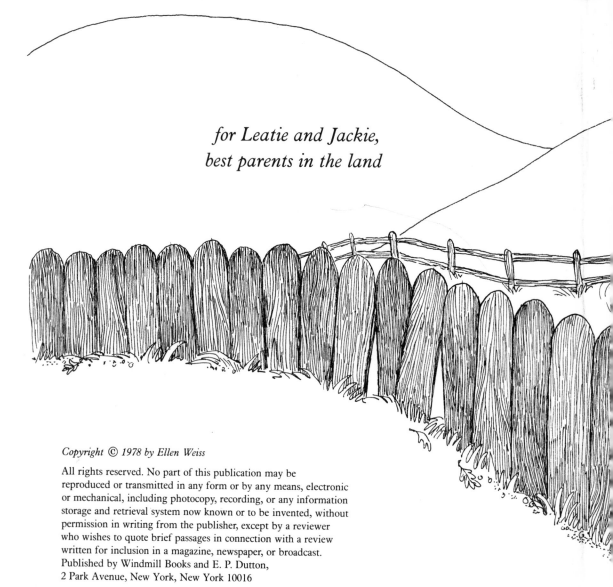

Library of Congress Cataloging in Publication Data
Weiss, Ellen.   Clara, the fortune telling chicken.

SUMMARY: A clever chicken tricks some sheep out
of their wool by telling them their fortunes and making
sure they come true.
    [1. Fortune telling—Fiction.   2. Sheep—Fiction.
3. Chickens—Fiction]   I. Title.
PZ7.W4472CL 1978   [E]   77-26198
ISBN 0-525-61576-8

Published simultaneously in Canada by Clarke, Irwin
and Company, Limited, Toronto and Vancouver

Edited by Robert Kraus

Printed in U.S.A.   First Edition

10 9 8 7 6 5 4 3 2 1

"**B**rrrr," shivered Clara as she opened
the gate of Woolly Sheep Farm. "This seems like
the perfect place for me. I do need a new wool shawl
to keep me warm this winter. But where *is* everybody?"

She peeked into the barn. "What a mess!" thought Clara. There, amid dirt, dust, and hay, were the most unhappy looking sheep she had ever seen.

"Baa, baa, *blah*!" moaned Simon. "Eat and sleep! Sleep and eat! Life is such a bore!"

"Ho hum! Hum-drum!" sighed Lilly. "No one here ever looks at me. I feel so lonely."

"Nothing to look forward to," complained Chester. "Only the long, cold winter. How dull!"

And they all turned away from each other and went back to sleep.

"Perfect!" thought Clara. "A fortune-teller's paradise! I see that I am needed here!"

"Step right up, my friends!" she sang. "Don't be afraid.
Come and see what surprises await you!" Her jewelry
jingled and jangled as she fluttered around the barnyard.

The sleepy sheep staggered out of the barn. They
could hardly believe their eyes.

"Who are you?" demanded Simon. "And what are you doing here?"

"I'm Madame Clara, the gypsy chicken. I travel here. I travel there. And I've come to tell your fortunes!"

"What's a fortune?" asked Blossom.

"It's what will happen to you today, tomorrow, or even next year," said Clara.

"We know what will happen," said Walter. "NOTHING!"

"Ah, my friends! I can tell you things you never
dreamed could happen to you. I can see it all in my
crystal ball. All I ask is a place to stay, some food
to eat, and a bit of wool from each of you."

"Oh, do stay, Madame Clara! Be our guest!" the sheep
cried. Then they all lined up to hear their fortunes.

"Ah ha! I see a handsome young sheep in your life,
Lilly. You will fall in love by the first snowfall."

"Who is he?" asked Lilly.

"You will have to find out for yourself," Clara replied.
And she snipped off Lilly's wool and put it in her bag.

"Ah, Trudy! You will live in a beautiful new home.
It will look like a palace!" said Clara.

"But, where is it?" asked Trudy.

"Look carefully and you will see it," said Clara,
and she snipped off some more wool.

"Chester! You will make many new friends," said Clara.

"Where will I find them?" asked Chester.

"Ah," said Clara. "They are closer than you think!
And her scissors went snip, snip, snip!

One by one the sheep went into Clara's tent.
And one by one they came out with their heads filled
with fabulous fortunes.

"Something wonderful is going to happen
to me soon!" giggled Blossom.
"By the first snowfall!" agreed Lilly.

"I'm much too excited to sleep," said Chester.

"I think I'll sweep the barn," said Trudy.

"I'll help you," said Blossom, and she sang a little tune. "I'll dust," said Walter, and he did a little dance.

The sleepy barnyard was suddenly buzzing with
activity. Clara watched them through the window as
they tidied up.

"Just as I planned," laughed Clara. "Now I can get some work done myself. I have enough wool to knit myself a complete winter wardrobe! Then, before the first snow falls, I'll be on my way." And she worked as fast as she could.

But the sky was getting gray. Suddenly, a few
snowflakes began to fall.

"Look!" shouted Simon. "It's snowing! This is our
lucky day!"

All the sheep rushed outside to celebrate the first snowfall.

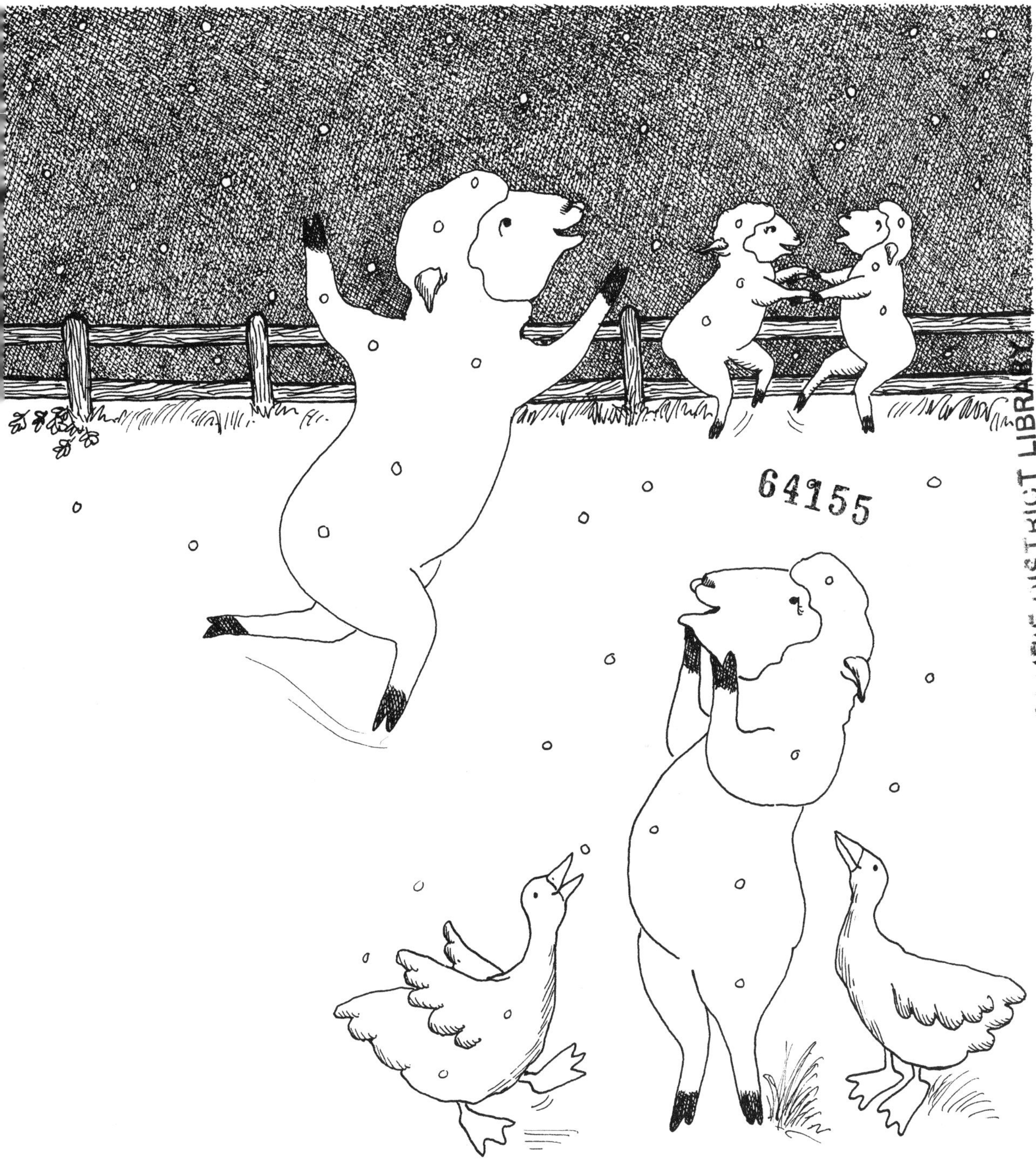

Then they sat down to wait for their fortunes to come true. They waited. And waited. And waited.

"How long must we sit here?" complained Blossom.

"I'm cold," shivered Lilly. "Keep me warm, Simon."

"I'm f-f-f-freezing," said Walter.

"I want my wool back!" shouted Chester.

"Clara tricked us!" said Trudy. "She's got our wool and we have nothing. Not one of our fortunes has come true!"

The cold, angry sheep marched toward Clara's tent.
Clara heard the commotion and looked outside.

"Oh, no!" said Clara. "The snow has fallen sooner
than I expected. I'd better think of something quick!"

"Ah, my friends," she clucked, "I've been expecting you. Your fortunes have come true!"

"No, Madame Clara. We are here to tell you—"

"Shhh. Say no more!" interrupted Clara. "Let me guess. Simon, you have fallen in love with Lilly."

Simon and Lilly looked at each other and blushed.

I told you it would happen!" said Clara. And now
you are *all* good friends! You really care about each other!"

"We just never tried before," said Chester.

"Blossom, I heard you singing. And Walter, I saw
you dancing. What fun you were having!"

"But where is the palace you promised?" demanded Trudy. "I don't see any palace!"

"Follow me," said Clara "and I'll show you." She led them all to the barn and opened the door.

"Look at this place," said Clara. You've turned an old dingy barn into a sparkling palace!"

"It's true!" they agreed. "You made it all happen, Clara!"

"But I see in my crystal ball that without your wool you would be cold all winter," said Clara.

"Amazing!" said Walter. "That's just what we came to tell you!"

Clara smiled mysteriously.

"I also see a new and wonderful way for you to keep warm."

She disappeared into her tent and returned with a
basket full of hats, scarves, sweaters, and booties.

"There's surely enough here for all of us!" said Clara.
"One shawl is all I need. The rest is my gift to you."

"How beautiful!" said all the sheep.
"Almost as warm as our very own wool."
"Oh, Clara—how can we ever thank you?"

But when they turned around, Clara was hurrying
down the road.

"Come back!" yelled Blossom. "We need you! Nothing good ever happened to us until you came."

"Nonsense!" called Clara. "Good fortune is all around you. All you have to do is look for it!"

Then she wrapped her new shawl around her and smiled. "Not a bad job for an old gypsy like me! Now, I wonder where my feet will take me next....!"